GhostHaunted

Valley Ghosts Series Book Two

BL Maxwell

BL Maxwell

Valley Ghosts Series Book Two

BL Maxwell

Copyright

GHOST HAUNTED

The Valley Ghosts Series

Editing provided by: Labyrinth Bound Edits

Warning

Intended for a mature an 18+ audience only. This book contains material that may be offensive to some and is intended for a mature, adult audience. It contains graphic language, explicit sexual content, and adult situations.

Dedication

Thanks to my beta readers, proofreaders, Labyrinth Bound Edits, and all the people in the October Burst of Paranormal Group. And especially thanks to all the people who love the paranormal as much as I do.

Chapter One

Dinner Date

We were going on our first date. We'd been friends for years, and in that time, we'd gone out numerous times together, but never as a couple. This was so new to us both. Wade and I had made it official after staying the weekend in a real haunted house and being scared half to death. After that weekend, admitting our feelings for each other wasn't quite as scary as we'd both imagined it would be.

Actually, we came clean to each other while we were in The Vineyard House and in fear for our very lives at the hands of the spirits that seemed to enjoy making their presence known. The ghosts of Louise and Robert Chalmers were not subtle in letting us know they were indeed present. Louise told us Wade was a powerful empath, and I was aware of spirits and they were drawn to me because they knew. We'd figure that out another time though.

My attention was pulled back to Wade. "So, where are we going again?"

"Nope, it's a surprise. I want you to enjoy the full experience," Wade teased.

"I've already enjoyed the 'full experience'. I'm not sure anything can top that. Although, the job in Old Sac might." I thought briefly about our meeting with our new client—well, our first real client—Dean Peterson, the manager of a restaurant in Old Sacramento that had been having strange activities they couldn't easily dismiss.

He thought about it for a second before he answered. "It's something we haven't done for a few years, but you used to like it. Hopefully, that hasn't changed."

I didn't want to admit it, even to Wade, but staying at The Vineyard House had changed me. While I was still interested in the paranormal, now I was afraid. I knew we could be hurt, and it was something I didn't want to happen again; not to me, and not to him.

"Okay, I give. Where are you taking me on our first date?"

"You'll see." He teased me again as he locked the door to his house and walked out to the car. I noticed Wade's mom standing in her yard watching us. She had the hose in her hand watering her flowers.

"Hi, Mrs. Rivers."

I could see her roll her eyes from across the yard.

"Jason, how many times do I have to tell you? You can call me Mom now." She smiled over at me. "Wade—"

"Bye, Mom. Gotta go."

He pulled me along by the hand, rushing to his car.

After waving to Wade's mom, we drove away before she could come over and give us the third degree. To say she was happy we were a couple was an understatement. She'd have us married tomorrow in her backyard if it was her choice. And if I was being honest, I was okay with that idea too.

"So, tell me where we're going?" I tried again.

He leaned in and kissed me as we stopped at a stop sign. "Nope, you'll just have to wait. But I will tell you we'll be going to dinner first."

"Really? Like a real date?"

"Yes, like a real date. It is a real date. You're my boyfriend, right?"

"Hell yes, I'm your boyfriend," I said with emphasis.

"Okay then, let your boyfriend take you out on a date." He winked at me before continuing to drive us to our destination. We ended up in downtown Sacramento and Wade pointed to one of the small local restaurants that Sacramento had plenty of.

"Oh, this place? It looks nice."

"Hopefully the food is good. I have it on good authority that it's promising," Wade commented.

"So, Jimbo recommended it?" I said with a raised brow as we drove around the block searching for a parking space. This area was not known for easy parking on any day of the week.

"Yep, he's the food expert in the group," Wade admitted.

"I still can't believe we're a group. Seriously, what's the chance we'd find someone like him out in the middle of nowhere?"

"He said he's trying to hire another cook so he's free to do more investigations with us. Apparently he's over his aversion to ghosts."

I turned to look at Wade before a loud laugh exploded out of me. "That asshole. First, he wants nothing to do with ghost hunting; now, he can't get enough."

"Yeah, he said he wants to branch out and start seeing more than the single street of Coloma," Wade continued.

"You sure it has nothing to do with Dean, the manager at The Hitching Post?"

"Oh, I'm pretty sure that's part of it. Has he told you anything more about that? I know there's more to that story."

Wade's brow furrowed in concentration. It really was a mystery to the two of us, what exact history was between Jimbo and Dean. Because there was something there, and Jimbo wasn't talking.

We finally found a space three blocks from the restaurant, and Wade parallel parked like a pro. We walked down the tree-lined street in the crisp fall weather. It was a perfect night so far and it had barely begun.

"So, have you gone on any dates with guys before?" he asked me, his voice full of curiosity.

"Nope, you're my first." I slow-blinked at him.

He stopped walking and faced me. "Seriously? I thought you said you'd been with other guys?"

"I have, just not on a date. Usually it was a hookup or someone I met when I was already out."

Wade thought about that for a second before speaking. "So, I really am your first?" He slid his hands down to my hips before pulling me into him.

My breathing sped up. I reached up to cradle his face. "You're my first boyfriend, my first boy date, my first best friend, and my first love. You're everything to me, Wade."

He leaned in and kissed me hard. I was lightheaded and drunk on his scent as he licked across my lips, and I opened to his probing tongue. I still couldn't believe this was real and Wade really wanted me as a boyfriend, but I was more than happy about it. Being in love with my best friend and knowing he loved me back was the best. And having him as a partner in our ghost hunting business was awesome. I still regretted every day I had let him believe I wasn't interested in him as anything more than a friend. If I could get those days back somehow, I'd do it in an instant.

"Hey, what's going on?"

He pressed his thumb into the crease of my brow. I reached up and took his hand before pressing a kiss to his palm. "Nothing, just playing shoulda, coulda, woulda. Nothing new." He gave me a troubled look but entwined our fingers and started walking.

It didn't take us long to get to the restaurant, a place that was part of the farm-to-fork movement in the area. We walked up to the hostess and waited for her to seat us. Once again, I thought how odd it was that, even though this was new to me, I was completely comfortable with being with Wade. That made me smile, just in time for us to be seated and have menus shoved at us both.

"This place is busy," I remarked as I watched the wait staff hustle around taking care of everyone in the small restaurant. We were lucky to be seated at an outside table, which was perfect on this night. And a little removed from the hustle and bustle inside.

"Yeah, Jimbo said it's one of the new up-and-coming places. I have no clue how he has time to keep up on this stuff, manage his own restaurant, and run around with us looking for ghosts."

"You said he's getting help, right?"

"He's trying, but he's so freaking picky, who knows if he'll actually let someone else take over or not. Might be easier for him to sell and open a new place in Sacramento."

"I can see him doing really well here."

"Enough about Jimbo. How was your week? I miss spending all of our time together." Wade smiled and covered my hand with his.

"It was good, same as always. I'm ready for the weekend and spending time with you."

"Me too. That's my favorite part of the week, the days we get together." Wade looked uncertain, apparently still not quite sure he could believe my feelings for him were real.

I leaned forward and pecked his lips. "Me too, babe. So what sounds good to you?"

We looked through the menu and decided to go with our usual. Burgers. These were a little more gourmet, with brie and arugula, but still burgers. We sat and enjoyed each other's company, the great weather, and tried to steal each other's fries. We'd known each other so many years, and shared countless meals together, but this one was different. The way he reached for my hand across the table, and the look in his eyes. Everything was different. Time seemed to fly by; before we knew it we'd finished eating, and made our way back to the car.

As soon as I closed my door Wade wove his fingers through my hair and pulled me in for a kiss. He licked along my lips and I opened to him. The warm glide of his tongue and the way he held me to him so tight made me want more. He pulled back enough to rest his forehead against mine. My heart raced and our breaths mingled together as I tried to form a coherent thought.

"So, homeward bound?" I asked.

"Nope, now for the good part."

"Oh my god, give me a clue. You're killing me here."

He laughed at that. "Nope, but we're close, so you'll find out soon enough."

We merged onto the freeway and drove a few exits down to a more industrial area. Then after a few turns, we ended up in a warehouse district. There were cars parked everywhere on both sides of street and all of the parking lots were packed.

"Wade, where are we? I've never been to this area before." Now I was nervous. I trusted Wade, but I was a little worried about where he was taking us.

"Just a minute and you'll see. Help me look for a parking space."

We drove down a few more streets, and just like at the restaurant, we got lucky and found a space on a side street. After parking, Wade opened his door and walked around to the back of the car.

"Come on, you'll love it."

"Will I? I have no clue what 'it' is," I snipped at him.

"Sure you do. He's the clown Pennywise," he said with a smirk, referencing the scary-as-fuck clown from the movie It. Fuck that, I might be fascinated by ghosts, but scary clowns? Hell, no.

"You know I hated that movie."

"Yes, but I don't understand why."

"I like ghosts, but not shit that's meant to scar me for life. I couldn't sleep for a week after I saw the first one, and the second wasn't much better."

He took my hand and led me down the street to where some giant spotlights lit up the sky.

"What is this?" I tried again, but as we turned another corner, I could see a line with a crowd of people waiting outside one of the warehouses. The spotlights were set up in front, but I still wasn't sure what it was. We joined the back of the line, only to have people walk right up behind us. There had to be a couple of hundred people lined up for whatever was inside this place. No music played, so I didn't think it was some super-secret party, but I still couldn't tell what it was or why Wade was so excited about keeping it a secret.

Chapter Two

Haunted What?

"So, what do you think?" I heard asked behind me. I turned around to see two guys a little younger than us. One had dark eyes and hair, while the other was blond and looked as confused as I felt.

"I'm not sure what I think yet. Are you sure we need to do this? I can think of about a hundred things I'd rather do," the blond guy answered.

"I'm with you, man," I interrupted.

The guy with the dark hair looked at me before laughing. "Don't encourage him. I had to practically drag him here as it was. I'm Rio, by the way. This is my boyfriend, Caden," he said with a smile as he held out his hand.

"Hey, good to meet you," I said as I shook hands with him. "I'm Jason, and this is my man, Wade." Wade rolled his eyes at me before shaking hands with Rio.

"How's it going?" Rio asked him.

"Good so far, as long as I can get Jason in the door, I think it'll be a lot of fun."

"Hey." I play-punched him in the arm before turning to face Rio and his boyfriend. "I still have no clue what we're even doing here. He won't tell me what this is."

Rio looked between us then at Caden before he bent in half in laughter. "Wait, so you didn't tell him what this is?"

"Nope," Wade popped his lips as he said it, before looking over at me with a sly grin.

"Does he like this kinda thing?" he asked.

"Normally. But under different circumstances," Wade said.

Once again, the Rio guy looked between the two of us and started laughing. His boyfriend stood there with a shy grin, obviously trying to not laugh at my expense but not really pulling it off.

I turned to Wade. "Okay, fucker, tell me what this is."

"You'll know in about five minutes. Hey, you guys want to go in with us? I have coupons."

"Sure, we have some too. Maybe we can share them with someone else."

We asked the people in front of us and they were glad to take them, but only needed three; we still had one left.

"Hey, assholes." Out of nowhere, Jimbo appeared. "What the fuck, Wade, I thought you were going to swing by the house and give me a ride? I had to Uber it over here."

"Sorry, man, I totally spaced it. You know how I get after I eat. And the place was great; thanks for the recommendation."

"So, they had good burgers?" Jimbo said, with an irritated look on his face.

"Yep, you know us too well," Wade answered with a grin.

Caden and Rio looked between us like they were watching a tennis match and waiting for something really exciting to happen. Wade was the first to snap out of it and introduce them to Jimbo. After shaking hands, the five of us continued to shoot the shit about nothing in particular.

"So, did you tell him yet?" Jimbo whisper-yelled at Wade.

"No, he hasn't told me shit. Why don't you tell me, Jimbo? Since you seem to know what we're here for." I tried to stare him down, but damn, Jimbo was master of the stare down. Maybe it had to do with the short buzzed hair, or more likely it was the chronic scowl.

"I'm not saying nothing. You'll know soon enough anyway," he snapped, finally breaking eye contact.

I realized the line had moved and we were within twenty feet of the entrance. I looked around, and finally, I could see a sign. Haunted House it read. I did a double and then a triple take. That couldn't be right. I slowly turned my head to look at Wade and Jimbo. They both locked eyes with me before busting up and falling all over each other.

"Wait, wait, so you can handle staying the weekend in a real haunted house, but this you're afraid of?" Jimbo taunted me—taunted!

"Fuck you, Jimbo. Who was the one that didn't want to even set foot in The Vineyard House?"

He looked at me and once again bent over laughing. Behind him, Caden and Rio continued to watch us like we were nuts or on drugs or just really weird.

Wade finally took pity on me and laid his arm over my shoulders before pulling me in close to him. "Sorry, babe, I knew if I told you earlier, you'd never want to go, and Jimbo and I really want to see it. It's almost Halloween. Come on, it'll be fun."

"What is it about Halloween haunted houses that you don't like anyway?" Jimbo asked once again. "I mean, it's all just smoke and mirrors. Not flying glass, salt, and candles."

"Nothing, it's nothing. It's just not my thing." I cleared my throat and tried to act casual and not let them know I was freaked out. I really fucking hated clowns, zombies, crazed lunatics—pretty much anything I knew was waiting for us in this shit show we were about to enter.

I took Wade's hand. If he was going to force me to do this, then dammit, he was going to suffer right along with me. He smiled at me and I knew he was loving every minute. He was scared half to death in most of the places we'd visited hunting for ghosts. But he wasn't afraid of any of the horror movies he forced me to watch. Holy shit, and now we were at a haunted house.

In the background I heard Wade and Jimbo talking to the two guys behind us, but all I could think about was what was waiting for us in the warehouse we were inching closer to.

Shit.

Chapter Three

Pitch Black

"Come on man, it won't be that bad. Right, Caden?" the dark-haired guy, Rio, promised.

"How do I . . . ? Right, what he said," Caden said as he rubbed his ribs where Rio had elbowed him.

We were now next in line to go in. The guy charging admission at the front of the line was dressed as a Steampunk-style funeral director. That wasn't so bad. I could handle this. He walked up to us and immediately got so close to me that if I moved, our noses would touch. He didn't move, just stared at me with his crazy eyes that had white contact lenses covering the irises.

"Hey, back off, dude." Wade made to shove him off me. But he held his ground.

"Who among you is brave enough to enter the house of horrors I have created? It has taken me years to amass this wonderful collection of ghouls and ghastly sights and sounds. It's not for the faint of heart, as it can cause that very heart to stop beating at any time during your visit. Not to worry though. If that does happen, I will gladly add you to our exhibit. I'm sure you'll make a wonderful, new . . . attraction." He dragged his finger down my cheek as he finished his little speech. Or warning? Maybe it was enough to make Wade want to leave.

I looked over to see him smiling from ear to ear. I looked past him to Jimbo, and he wore the same big smile. Apparently I was the only one who didn't want to enjoy the tour. Wade paid for us to enter, and we moved forward as a group, Rio and Caden tagging along with us.

"How many of you are brave enough to enter into the zone of no return? How many?" He backed off a little but still kept up the dramatics. He was wearing a ratty top hat with goggles resting on the brim and clothes that looked like he'd been buried in them around a hundred years ago. His face was painted to look like a skeleton, but he had pieces of flesh that had been torn away, revealing the muscles in his jaw.

God, I hated this shit already. Wade took my hand and kissed me on the cheek.

"Come on, let's get this party started," Wade joked.

"Is that what the teenagers are calling it these days?" I deadpanned.

He turned around to the two guys behind us. "So, is that what the kids are saying these days?"

"Man, we're almost twenty, so I'm not sure which kids you're talking about," Rio shot back.

"All righty, then. Gentlemen, shall we go on in?" Wade said to all of us. "You guys want to stick with us?"

Rio and Caden looked at each other. "Sure, let's do this," Caden said.

We moved as a group toward the front entrance, with the weird guy in the top hat leading the way.

"Come on, everyone, stay together. You don't want to get left behind. Stragglers will be eaten. Bwaahahahahaha," he called out, his one last warning.

"Oh god," I groaned.

He slid open a heavy door and waited for us to walk inside and then slammed it shut. It was so fucking dark in there that I grabbed the nearest hand to me, hoping it was Wade, but not really caring.

"What the fuck? Whoever is holding my damn hand needs to let go now."

"Fuck you, Jimbo." I felt around for another hand but instead found a denim-covered crotch.

"Dude!" One of the other guys said that. I wasn't sure if it was Caden or Rio.

"Sorry, sorry. I can't see shit, and I'm freaking out. Wade, where the fuck are you?"

"I'm right here, babe," he said from my left. I groped in that direction and grabbed his hand like my life depended on it, then the lights went on and a strobe light started flashing. We cringed away from it and everyone laughed in relief.

A woman dressed as a zombie bride, complete with exposed chest bones and a partially exposed skull, came dragging herself through a door I hadn't seen. I pulled Wade in front of me to keep her away.

"Thanks, man." He looked back at me but stayed between me and the zombie. This was new; usually he was behind me. I started to smile, but then the bride continued toward us until she forced us back against the door.

A door slid open behind her and she dragged herself over to the opening. And I mean that literally, her leg was dragging behind her dress. I squeezed Wade's hand a little tighter and felt Jimbo behind me urging me forward.

The walls in this area were painted with fluorescent paint, giving it an eerie green glow in the black lights which were hidden all over the area. Sugar skulls were placed around what looked like an old cemetery; there were gravestones, mounded dirt that looked like fresh graves, and suddenly the place was filled with fog. The glow of the lights made it look even creepier.

I clenched Wade's hand tighter than I probably should have, but still not tight enough to make me relax, as we slowly inched forward. Suddenly one of the mounds of dirt started moving, and a hand burst out of it.

"Jason, dude, chill out. It's all pretend." Jimbo both teased and tried to reassure me at the same time.

"I know it's pretend, but it's creepy as hell." The whole time the dirt kept moving off the mound, and all at once, someone sat up in the mound/grave. He was covered in dirt and grime and looked decayed and rotted.

Wade dropped my hand and walked up to the living corpse. "Hey, man, need a hand?" He held his hand out, offering some help. The corpse slowly turned his head and looked at Wade's hand before holding out his own, which was mostly bone and rotting flesh.

Wade pulled his hand back quickly. "Ew, no thanks. Sorry, man." The corpse looked at him and gave him a creepy, toothy grin before lying back in his grave again.

We continued to move forward and took in the different graves and the offerings that were for Día de los Muertos. Everything looked so real. There were several more of the living dead that had apparently come back to visit their living relatives.

"This is kinda cool. Not too creepy and not bloody," I said to Wade.

"I told you it was fun. Come on, let's move on to the next room." He tugged me forward, and we went through some plastic sheeting that was draped between the two rooms. The next room was very different and looked more like a hospital room.

I knew immediately I wasn't going to like this room one bit.

Chapter Four

Lunatics, Vampires, and Blood

We entered what looked like a lab. There were numerous containers boiling or bubbling with flames burning under them. Lab equipment was scattered around the room, but it was in disarray. Like something bad had happened here, and what had survived, endured some sort of struggle.

We moved a little farther into the room and saw an operating table that was tilted up and away from us so we couldn't see exactly what—or who—was on it. By now we were in a pretty tight group; no one wanted to be left behind on their own, and no one was being brave and going ahead of everyone else to check it out.

As we got nearer to the operating table, it was obvious there was something, or someone, on it. When we were close enough, we saw a beast that resembled a werewolf being dissected: his skin pulled back and held open with nails and other instruments, exposing all of his organs. His heart still beat while his lungs expanded rapidly. I looked up at his face, and he turned to look at me with a big, wolfish grin.

"Sick! Oh my god, what the hell is this shit?" Jimbo asked.

It really was gross—and amazing. It looked very real and very nasty. We tried to continue out of the room, but then someone in a lab coat rushed past us and went immediately to the wolf on the table. I didn't look to see what he did, but whatever it was, the wolf started growling at him before snapping and trying to pull himself free from the nails and instruments holding him pinned to the table.

The doctor, or whatever the hell he was, turned to give us an evil grin, and even he looked crazy as hell. I pushed my face into Wade's shoulder, hoping for a small break from the sensory overload and the major adrenaline rush I was experiencing.

He kissed the top of my head and rubbed my arm while encouraging me to keep moving forward. We passed through another panel of plastic sheets, and this time we ended up in what looked like a back alley. It was dark, and low fog made it appear even more menacing. Wade tugged me forward, and we walked on.

The alley was fairly long, maybe twenty yards, but narrow. And it appeared there was only one way to go. We walked as a group toward the other end, when suddenly a woman came busting through what, for us, would be the exit, screaming at the top of her lungs.

"Help me, someone please help me." Her eyes locked on us, and she ran at us with a panicked look on her face. "Can you guys help me? Some lunatic is chasing after me. I don't know what he wants and I . . ."

That was all she got out before a silhouette of a man appeared out of nowhere right behind her. She froze for a second, her face a mask of true terror. He grabbed her from behind, and with one hand on her forehead and the other wrapped around her waist, he pulled her to him.

She screamed once again, loud and terrifying. We ducked at the sound and started to rush to her. Then the man behind her made eye contact with us. He was handsome, in a dark, macabre way, with eyes that looked black in the dim lights. He slowly leaned down and bit her neck. Blood ran down her chest and arm in rivulets of deep crimson. He raised his head and a rush of blood ran from his mouth and gushed from her open wound.

We cringed back from the scene as he shoved her to the side and she crumpled in a heap. He curled his hands into claws and rushed toward us. Some of us screamed, and we tried to turn and run at the same time, only to find that our way was blocked by the woman who had been bitten. Now she snarled at us and showed her teeth. Blood covered her everywhere and continued to spurt out of the wound in her neck.

We panicked and tried to run back the way we'd come; the vampire was no longer there. "Come on, haul some ass everyone," Wade yelled, and we immediately obeyed.

We burst out the end of the alley into another room. This one was well lit, and with hieroglyphics written on it, it looked like the entrance to a pyramid. While I was glad we were out of the dark alleyway, I was pretty sure what awaited us next was no better. I looked over at Wade, who was grinning from ear to ear.

"Are you having fun? This is amazing, don't you think?" He talked a mile a minute, barely taking a breath in between.

"Oh yeah, this is great. My heart hasn't exploded yet, so I'm calling it a win."

Caden looked over at Rio and bent over laughing. "You guys are so fun. I'm so glad we went in with you."

"Easy, mí amor. I'm not so sure Jason's enjoying it as much as Wade is," Rio leaned into him and said quietly. Probably hoping I didn't hear.

"You two are just as bad as these guys." I pointed my finger at them both and then thumbed back at Wade and Jimbo. "I don't understand how you think this is fun."

The four of them paused for a second before once again laughing at me.

"You're so funny when you're scared," Jimbo had to add.

"Fuck you, Jimbo. I'm going to remember this when we're on our next job."

That sobered him a little . . . just a little. "Screw you, Jason. You know I can handle it." He nodded to punctuate what he'd said. Even though we both knew it was a lie.

Wade and I locked eyes then, and we laughed at him. He'd stuck around and made it through The Vineyard House, but it was with constant complaint and threats of mutiny.

Just then a group of kids ran past us. Little kids, maybe ten or eleven years old. They were laughing and looking around the room like it was the best place they'd ever been to. They pushed past us, some of them giving us annoyed looks, like we should just get out of their way and let them get on with their fun. They didn't even hesitate to burst through the door into the pyramid at the end.

Rio and Wade both shrugged their shoulders. Wade took my hand again, and we started walking toward the end where who knew what was waiting for us.

Chapter Five

Mummies and Guardians of the Dead

We walked through the entrance that was made to look like the stone blocks of a pyramid and into a large area that was well lit. It didn't seem nearly as terrifying as what we'd already been through. There were two Anubis at both sides of the entrance holding their staffs. I stopped to look at them closer. They were more like zombies: part of their flesh was rotted away and they had the remnants of mummy wraps hanging off them.

We walked farther into the room and realized it was a shooting gallery in the middle.

"Now this I can handle," I said.

"Let's see how many mummies we can shoot," Wade said.

We walked up to join the line that had formed. This really looked fun. It was a laser light shooting gallery, and it was huge. There were so many moving targets it was hard to keep track of them. Wade came up behind me and put his hands on my hips and his chin on my shoulder.

"How's it going, babe?"

"This I can handle. That other shit, not so much."

He stuck out his bottom lip in a pout. "You don't like our first date."

"Are you kidding? I love our first date. It's the zombies and vampires I'm not loving. And don't even get me going on the blood and other horrible things I've seen tonight."

He rested his forehead between my shoulder blades, and I turned to face him. I ducked down, forcing him to make eye contact.

"I love you. I love you no matter where you take me. Even if we end up in another real haunted house, I'll still love you."

He lifted his head with a smile. "I love you too, and I knew you'd end up loving it here."

I shoved him back before grabbing the front of his shirt and pulling him back to me. I took his face in my hands and kissed him until everything in the background faded away. Until there was only us, and none of the scary stuff mattered. "I love you. But I'd rather not go to another haunted house unless it's the real kind."

"Yeah, yeah, you two. Get a room or go home or somewhere, anywhere else than where I am," Jimbo grumbled.

"Fuck you, Jimbo," we said in unison before laughing at him.

Finally it was our turn. We found an empty space, and I leaned down on the counter, getting ready to aim at whatever target popped up.

"I'll bet you a beer I can hit more zombies than you," Wade wagered.

"You're on. You know I'm gonna kick your ass." I clapped him on the back as I got ready for the round to start.

A buzzer sounded and the targets started popping up out of random places where I didn't expect there to be anything. For ninety seconds, we were focused on what we could shoot at, with the occasional shove to try to distract each other from doing too good in the competition.

Mummies of all types popped up and snarled or blew out a dusty breath before disappearing, only to have another appear in a different area. A huge stone sarcophagus slid open, and a mummy that was more decaying bones than wraps sat up and snarled at us.

By the time the round had ended, we were laughing and having a great time, even the new guys that had tagged along with us.

"You ready to go into the next room?" Wade asked. "I think it's zombies."

"What's the difference between a zombie and a mummy? I mean, besides the bandages." I felt my brows furrow as I tried to figure it out myself.

"One is wrapped up and is from Egypt," Jimbo added the obvious.

"But they're both zombies . . . technically," I mused.

"Yeah, but at least with a mummy, his mouth is wrapped up. Makes it harder for him to eat your brain," Wade added with an evil glint in his eyes.

"Thanks for that visual," I teased him with a shove. "Let's get this over with. Hopefully there're no clowns. Man, I hate clowns the most."

"Don't worry, I'll protect you from the scary clowns if we see any," Wade volunteered.

"You're not making me feel any better about this."

"I know. Come on, let's move on to the next section." Wade led us along.

We made our way to the large sliding door at the other end of the room. It had a video screen on the wall with hands that looked like they were scratching at the screen to get out, making it look like people trying to escape from the other side. I stood for a second and stared at it.

"Zombies. Fuck, I was hoping you were joking."

"Nope. Shall we?" Wade offered with a sweep of his hand in the direction of the zombies.

Chapter Six

The Living Dead

"Hell yes, we shall," Jimbo piped up, pushing past us to grab the handle of the door.

As soon as he slid it open, there was a crash of activity as a group of people tried to rush back to get away from whatever was in the room.

"Shit," Rio shouted, "what the fuck?"

We tried to back up to give them space, but there were people behind us too. They had no choice but to go back in the room. Two of the girls were crying, and the guys in the group didn't look too happy about having to go back in there.

As soon as they were clear of the outer door, they passed into what we could now see was an inner door. The five of us walked into the small area between the two doors. We looked around, and it was made to look like a place that was in ruin. Trash littered the floors and the walls were torn up; some had blood smeared on them, adding to the scare factor immensely.

Then the inner door started to open, and Wade grabbed for my hand.

"Fuck," I heard from someone in our group, likely Jimbo.

All at once the door was shoved open when a group of the undead advanced on us. There were maybe seven. They were horrible looking, flesh hanging off some of them. Some in stages of decay like they'd been dead for months, while others seemed fresh, with blood still oozing from their wounds.

They made a horrible groaning sound as they walked up to each of us and acted like they were going to attack us. We did what the first group did; Caden and Rio were at the door trying to claw at it to get it open, but it didn't budge. They gave up, and Caden covered his head while Rio jumped in front of him to try to ward off the zombie that looked intent on scaring them both half to death.

Wade, Jimbo, and I were smashed against the wall, hoping they forgot about us once they had an easy target in Caden and Rio.

No such luck. They turned to us and were in our faces. Biting, snarling, blood and nasty black ooze dripping down their chins from their decaying mouths. I knew it was fake, but wow, it looked real. My heart was about to pound out of my chest when some guy came running into the room with a shotgun.

"Everyone, get behind me," he directed.

We immediately did what he said. Not even thinking about where he might be leading us. He fired his gun twice at the zombies and they backed off enough for us to get over to where he stood.

"Come on, this way," he shouted again.

We followed him down the hall, away from the door. It had to be better than the zombies. I turned to look back and they were following us. I hoped they were the slow zombies, not the ones that could run, because I was about to break into a run and get the fuck out of there.

Wade took my hand and seemed to have the same idea because he was speed-walking next to me, and Jimbo was trying his best to keep up. Caden and Rio were behind us and were squeezed as close to us as they could get without causing us to stumble and fall. None of us wanted that to happen.

The guy that had saved us ran through an opening and was gone. Almost instantly there were zombies everywhere. Big, small, zombies of all sizes and degrees of deterioration. It was horrible, and it was terrifying. We broke out in a run going the same way the other guy had.

Only where the door had opened for him, now it was shut. There was no handle, and when I looked back, the hoard of zombies was slowly making their way toward us.

"Open up," Rio yelled.

"Fuck, what do we do?" Jimbo asked.

We were frantic, feeling around every surface for a lever or handle, something that would open a door. When we found nothing, I started wondering if we should be looking for weapons. This was some crazy shit.

"Tell me again why you wanted this to be our first date?" I yelled over at Wade. I was frantic to get out of this place.

"Just remember, none of it's real." He smiled over at me just before one of the zombies grabbed him from behind and dragged him over to the side. The wall tipped open, and they rolled him into it.

"Hey! What did you do with Wade? Where is he?" Jimbo was to the left of me and Rio and Caden were to my right. The zombies had us pinned against a wall made of corrugated metal. They inched closer to us, and just when I thought they were going to eat our brains—or do something equally horrible, I had no clue—the whole wall slid open and we tumbled into another room. The panel slid silently shut behind us. Plunging us once again into the unknown.

Chapter Seven

Ghosts of Halloween Past

Wade approached. "Hey, you guys okay?" He smiled at us while reaching to give me a hand up.

"Fucking fabulous," Jimbo snarked.

"Everyone okay?" I asked Rio and Caden. They looked at each other before nodding in reply.

"Let's figure out how to get out of here." We fanned out, searching for an exit from the small room we now found ourselves in. The lighting was dim, so it made it hard to make out any details. I wasn't able to see anything other than walls and a floor. There was plastic draped from the ceiling, giving the room an even creepier look.

I heard music playing very softly through the wall. "Shh, do you guys hear that?" I leaned in closer to see if that was really where it was coming from.

Everyone froze and listened. The sound of an organ could be heard, but it was hard to tell exactly where the sound was coming from.

It didn't seem to be playing an actual song, just random notes that sounded creepy as hell. I made eye contact with Wade. "You hear that?"

"Yeah, I hear it," he answered.

I looked at the other guys and they nodded too. Everyone was on edge. The past hour had made us work as a team. It was now us against whatever was behind that wall. I wasn't sure I was ready for it, as an opening was revealed.

We took a step back and everyone seemed to brace for what would be there. When it was wide open, it revealed what looked like an old house's interior. There was a huge fireplace in the center of the room, surrounded by various furniture that looked like it'd seen better days.

I looked at Wade, and he nodded for us to go in. It was a deserted room; we spread out to check out everything that was in the space. I was closest to a table, so I walked closer and looked at everything that was scattered on it. It looked like a séance had taken place here. Some tarot cards, a small crystal ball, a chicken foot—weird—and a few dead flowers were on the table.

Out of the corner of my eye, I saw movement. A sort of shimmer . . . no, it couldn't be. I kept my eyes on that area while walking toward Wade, who stood staring at one of the paintings on the wall.

"Wade," I whispered. "Do you see that?"

He looked at me before looking in the direction I was motioning to. I knew he had seen it when his eyes widened.

"Hey guys, over there," he said to the rest of the group.

We watched as several spirits seemed to take form as they walked through the wall. They must have been holograms, I kept telling myself, but they looked amazingly real.

They walked over to the table, three women and a man. They each took a seat, and one of the women started talking very animatedly while swirling her hands around the crystal ball.

We were mesmerized. Suddenly the crystal ball lit up and mist swirled around inside it. The spirit who was holding her hands above it reacted, throwing her head back and moving her mouth as though she were saying a silent incantation.

Suddenly the lights went off. We were plunged into darkness so black that I couldn't tell if my eyes were open or closed. I blindly felt around, and without thinking, I grabbed the closest hand I came in contact with. I clenched it tight and it clenched back just as fiercely.

"I hope that's you, Jason," Wade said from my right.

I looked his way but still wasn't able to see anything.

"Nope, I'm over here," I answered.

"What the?" Wade seemed to move around; I heard the scraping sound of shoes and soon felt hands at my waist.

"Sorry, babe, I thought you were right next to me," Wade said, from behind me

"If that's not your hand, then who the hell is it?" I asked as I turned to my left.

Suddenly the lights flashed back on, and there were other people in the room now besides the five of us. They looked as stunned as we did. I made eye contact with a guy who looked familiar, but I wasn't sure where I would know him from. I immediately pulled away from his grip.

"What the fuck, dude?"

"Hey, I just grabbed for the nearest hand. Not my fault it was the wrong one," the guy tried to explain.

Wade still gripped my hips as he looked between the two of us.

"Wait, you're Jason, right?" the stranger asked as he snapped his fingers and pointed at me in recognition.

"Yeah, do I know you?"

"Remember me? We met at a club about a year ago."

He was vaguely familiar. The other guys were watching me, waiting for me to respond.

"I thought I recognized you. How's it going, man?" I shook his hand and stepped a little closer to Wade. "This is my boyfriend, Wade."

He smiled warmly at us both. "Nice to meet you, Wade. I'm going to get back to my friends. Nice to see you again, Jason."

He looked at me a little longer than was comfortable before walking off to the next area.

I took Wade's hand and headed for what I thought was the door when the lights went out again.

Only this time the room was filled with spirits. They moved around in a frenzy, swirling around like a tornado of lost souls. The noise they made was horrible. Terrifying screams and wails that could be heard over the sound of wind blowing through the room. It seemed to catch everything in it, moving the furniture, blowing anything away that wasn't nailed down.

Wade pulled me to him, and we both tried to back away from most of the wind. Jimbo, Caden, and Rio followed suit. Just as quickly as it began, it ended. We were once again alone in the room. The tornado of spirits was nowhere to be found, and the door at the end slid open, inviting us to go that way.

As we moved to exit the room, Wade moved in closer.

"Who was that?" he whispered in my ear.

"I'm not sure, but I think it might have been a ghost of bad hookups past."

He laughed at that and kissed me on the cheek. Just as we were about to leave the room, I noticed a little girl spirit standing right next to the door waving at us. I waved back at her and shrugged my shoulder at the puzzled look Wade gave me. We continued through the door to the left.

Once again, we were in a hall.

"Is this almost done?" Caden asked. "I'm not sure how much more I can take."

"I have no clue. They didn't give us a map or tell us what to expect, so I guess it's either suck it up and endure it, or beg to leave early," Wade explained.

"I hope the next is the last. This is too creepy for me. I thought it was going to be fun, not scare the shit out of us," Jimbo added his own snarky comment.

"It is called a haunted house experience. So, you should be thankful it's only an experience and not real," Wade scolded.

Jimbo waved him off. "Whatever, Wade, this was your brilliant idea, not mine. I just went along so Jason wouldn't be so scared."

I looked between the two of them and couldn't hold back the laugh that burst out of me.

"Come on, let's see what's next."

Chapter Eight

It Had to be Clowns

We walked through what felt like a maze. The hallway narrowed and we seemed to walk back and forth without going anywhere. Then we walked down a long, narrow hall that appeared to run the length of the building, which was huge. Then the walls and floor started to change. Where they had been painted stark black, it was now the bright colors of glow-in-the-dark paint.

We walked around the last corner and it looked like the entrance to a circus tent. How bad could a circus be compared to the other freaky things we'd seen?

We entered as a group and took a seat on one of the benches set up around what looked to be a ring in the middle. Other people filed in around us. It seemed like this was sort of a gathering place for everyone who was taking in the event.

I glanced around and everyone else seemed as nervous as I felt. I hoped it was just a normal circus act, not some weird shit. Or clowns.

Music started to play, but not regular music. It sounded like a calliope that had been rolled down a hill a few times. It had a warped quality to it that made it even creepier, droning on with its broken melody, ramping up the creepy factor.

There were a few teens present, trying to look brave, but the cracks in their armor were starting to show. If they'd gone through the rooms we had, they had to be on edge. I reached for Wade's hand, thankful to feel him squeeze mine back.

This was pretend, but it was still scary as hell. I looked over at Wade and he smiled at me before I lay my head on his shoulder. I glanced past him to see Caden and Rio, heads bent together in a quiet conversation. Both of them wore warm smiles and looked incredibly in love. Then I looked past them to see Jimbo. The chronic look of impatience was written all over his face. I couldn't stop the laugh that burst out of me.

"Hey, Jimbo, how's it going, man?" I leaned forward to ask him.

He folded his arms across his chest and leaned back on the bench before crossing his ankles. "If there's clowns in this part, I'm leaving." He kept his eyes on the center ring the whole time he talked and never looked away from it.

"Yeah, I'm not a fan of clowns either." The words had no sooner left my mouth than a bunch of clowns came running out from behind a curtain. They didn't stay in the ring though. They continued on up into the rows of people. They were all sizes: big, small, short, tall, and all of them were messed up in some way. There were maybe twenty of them, but some were huge; they took up a lot of space and made it feel too close for comfort in the relatively small area.

Most of them had blood running from their mouths or dripping from their sharp teeth. Their eyes . . . it was like staring into the face of evil itself. I was ready to bolt when I turned and looked at Jimbo. His face had paled, and he was clenching the bench so tight his knuckles were white.

He slowly turned and made eye contact with me. I looked at Wade, and without another word, we jumped up and bolted for the door.

Only the door was closed now. We ran along behind the benches searching for another exit—there had to be one—but we were not having any luck. I still had Wade's hand crushed in mine and was close to dragging him along behind me.

"Wait, Jason, slow down," he shouted to me.

I couldn't slow down. I needed to get the hell out of there, and it needed to happen immediately. I saw that Caden and Rio were right there with us. Rio seemed a little worried now. He'd been so calm and easy-going. Seeing that worried me even more.

Some of the clowns noticed us and ran toward us. One had a huge head that was misshapen like it was formed of clay and had been dropped a few times.

My eyes went wide and I dropped Wade's hand. Now I was full-out running. There was no way I was staying to find out what those damn clowns had in store for us. A couple of them caught up to me and cornered me against the wall. I looked to my left and Wade was there too, with Jimbo on the other side.

"Hey, guys, over here," I thought I heard Rio call.

I looked past Jimbo and saw Rio waving frantically. There, just to the side of him, was an exit door. I grabbed Wade's arm and pulled him toward it. Jimbo was right behind us. I was beginning to panic. The clowns were still running around the area, some cornering groups of people and taunting them with their gnarly hands and bloody teeth.

When I was almost to the door, a clown stepped right in front of the opening to block it. And not just any clown. The one from that movie that will not be named that left me unable to sleep for at least two weeks when I was a kid.

"Oh shit," Wade shouted.

He jumped in front of me and Jimbo hid behind me. I couldn't blame him; he was as freaked out as I was.

"Go around him," Caden shouted. Both he and Rio waited for us by the door. Neither of them appeared to want to move away from it. Probably worried it would close again and we'd never get out of here.

Wade took my hand. "Ok, weird clown, we're gonna move around you and get out of here. So, just leave us alone, okay?" He tried to reason . . . with the clown.

"Wade, I don't think he gives a shit if we get out of here," I squeaked out through gritted teeth.

"Wade, less talking and more running," Jimbo yelled, while he gave me a little shove into Wade.

"Let's go!" I yelled and tried to drag Wade toward the door.

The clown advanced on us, slow and steady. Taking his time, like he was stalking his next victim and he wanted to make it last. He raised his hands into claws, and his smile grew bigger, more deadly. He zeroed in on Wade, forcing us to slowly back away. Jimbo clenched the back of my shirt, his hand shaking.

It was too much. The Vineyard House was terrifying, but this was so in your face. It was too real. I pressed my face to the center of Wade's back and he reached back and pulled my hand to his chest, forcing me even closer to him. He paused for a second and stopped moving.

"Hey, back off, asshole. This is supposed to be fun, not make us end up in counseling," Wade shouted.

The clown stopped, he tilted his head to the side, and his smile slowly faded.

"Sorry, man, I got a little carried away. Go on, start heading to the door and I'll give you some cover from the other guys." The clown spoke in a totally normal, totally human voice.

As soon as he said it, I felt better. At least now we could focus on getting out of here. I lifted my head and saw that Rio and Caden were pretty close to us, but still far enough away that they probably hadn't heard the clown break character.

Caden slowly turned away from the clown to face me, still darting his gaze at the clown, probably to keep track of where he was. He shook his head slightly, and nudged Rio to move in our direction.

The clown gave us a little wave, and we high-tailed it to the door. As soon as we were through, it slammed shut. The five of us sagged against it momentarily before springing away. No way in hell did we want to spend any more time in there than we already had.

We walked quickly to the other side of the room we now found ourselves in, far away from the door to the clown room. We looked around trying to see where to go next. It couldn't be worse than clowns. Could it?

Chapter Nine

Demons and Hellfire

We walked down a hall that got hotter and hotter the further we went. The walls took on the look of flames. Soon I could hear the sounds of metal clanking or heavy chains being slowly dragged along the floor.

By now we were leery of what would be next. Caden and Rio were still behind us, but they were now glued to each other's side, and both looked to be on high alert for anything that could jump out at us from any direction.

Jimbo was closer to me than I was comfortable with. He didn't have anyone else to clench onto, so I guessed he just needed that closeness to quell some of his own nerves.

I had yet to loosen the death grip I had on Wade's hand. He was clenching my hand just as tight, so the fear must have been mutual.

This whole experience so far had been way freakier than I would've expected. We'd been to haunted house attractions almost every year when we were kids. We both loved them, and the scares were exciting, but not terrifying.

This place was on a whole different level. The breaks in between scares were so few and far between that my body was on a constant adrenaline rush. I could feel my hands and legs shaking as we made our way down the hall.

While it was getting hotter and hotter, it was also getting brighter. It looked like open flames were now burning on both sides of the hall. The sound of metal clanking and dragging was getting nearer.

Suddenly we heard a guttural laugh that sounded like it came from some invisible giant. The sound was so loud and deep it made the floors vibrate under our feet. And seemed to come from everywhere. We stopped immediately and looked around for its source. But all there was for us to see were narrow hallways lined with flames.

"Come on, let's see what's next," Wade encouraged.

"I have a bad feeling about this," I said.

"Can't be worse than what we've already seen," he said.

"Can't it?"

He stopped then and turned to face me. Jimbo backed off a little to give us some space.

"Do you want to leave? I think we can find an attendant and tell them we've had enough and want out," Wade offered, giving me an escape.

"No, I want to finish. It's fun."

"Didn't feel like fun when we were running from those freaky clowns."

I smiled at him and traced his jaw. "I know, but I fucking hate clowns. And those were awful. Come on, let's see what else we need to survive to get out of here."

"Are you sure? I really wanted this to be fun, not torture."

"I'm sure, and you had no way of knowing how crazy this place was."

"I'm sorry," he said as he leaned his forehead against mine. "I wanted our first date to be special. We've done this so many times in the past, I just wanted it to be special with the two of us together."

"It's special. It's always special doing things with you. I think it always has been."

"Are you sure? I don't want you to feel like you have to stay when you really want to go."

"Oh, I want to go. But I'm making myself stay because, how am I going to be a good paranormal investigator if I can't make it through a fake haunted house?" I finally admitted my fear.

He looked me right in the eyes. "What you did was amazing at The Vineyard House. Don't ever think I don't realize that. It was terrifying and I'm so glad both of us got out of there in one piece. I was worried that might not happen."

"You mean the three of us, right, Wade?" Jimbo questioned from behind my back.

"Privacy," Wade scolded.

I didn't have to look at Jimbo to feel the scowl he was shooting Wade. He really had no boundaries, something we both loved and hated about him. It was just how he was, and we'd take him after going through the same things as us at The Vineyard House. He was one of us now, whether he liked it or not.

I walked past Wade before turning and tugging on his hand. "You ready?"

"I am if you are."

I looked to Jimbo, Rio, and Caden. Jimbo rolled his eyes, while the other guys nodded. We were trying to put up a brave front, but we were all scared.

I led us the rest of the way down the hall to a huge, heavy, metal door with giant rivets in it that glowed red, like the metal was still hot from recently being forged.

I slowly reached for the handle that was so big I couldn't reach all the way around it. Wade stopped me with a hand on my arm.

"Let me go first," he offered.

"No, it's okay," I insisted.

I pulled on the door, and it was as heavy as it looked. Mist oozed out. It was red and had a sulfur smell. A light flashed intermittently around the room, so I couldn't get a clear picture of everything that was in there.

Three people were tied to posts and being tortured. One looked as if he were being flayed alive. His head thrown back in an agonizing scream while a demon laughed and slowly tore his skin from his body.

This part was all fake. It had animatronic characters, and even though the images it portrayed were disturbing, it was obviously not real. We continued on to another chamber of the big center room where a man was being stretched on a table while a huge blade swung closer and closer to his abdomen. His eyes were huge as he tried to wiggle away from it.

The sound of footsteps got closer as we passed every room; the chains seemed to be dragging right next to us on a stone floor. The sound was nearly deafening now. Metal clanging, the blast of what sounded like a huge furnace blowing out flames, so many sounds of pain and torture it blended together into a giant wall of sound.

As we turned the corner into the last chamber, it was set up for a banquet, but the feast laid out was horrible: rotting flesh, dismembered bodies, goblets filled with blood. Demons of every conceivable shape writhed and danced around the table. Some of them chewed aggressively on human bones while others tore pieces of flesh from the bodies on the table. They chanted something in what sounded like some ancient language. Or at least a language I had never heard.

Stomping around to the far side of the room was what looked like a Minotaur. It was enormous, standing at least three feet taller than anything else in the room, and its hooves kept stomping in either annoyance or anger. It wore heavy, metal wristbands, and a chain was wrapped around its neck and dragging on the ground. The sound of it was piped into the room, making the chain appear to actually be heavy and cumbersome. Out of its head there were two large black horns that looked both terrifying and dangerous. It was an animatronic exhibit, but that knowledge didn't make it any less intimidating.

It must have had motion detectors, because when we walked into the area, it turned in our direction. It then pushed its chest out before bellowing. It was so loud and terrifying all of us jumped.

"I want to get out of here," I said to Wade, trying to sound calmer than I felt.

"Yeah, okay." We turned to leave the room, and the huge metal door slammed shut. What was up with this place and locking people in?

The Minotaur or demon or whatever it was stomped its way toward us. It was so big that every step sounded like it weighed a ton. It towered over us. The flames that were scattered around ignited into bigger blazes, simultaneously, causing a flash of heat we could all feel.

The five of us stood next to the door pounding to be let out. I turned just in time to see the Minotaur start to run toward us.

"Holy shit!" I shouted. Everyone turned to watch as it picked up speed. We ducked at the same time, and I covered my head, bracing for impact.

But none ever came. I peeked out through my arms to see it veer off and slam its horns into the wall to the right of us. The door slid open like it had never been shut, and we tumbled out.

"Dudes, I don't know how much more I can take," Jimbo confessed. "I thought this would be fun, but I'm pretty freaked out."

I brushed myself off and stood next to Wade. "Ready to see what's next?"

Chapter Ten

Healing Hearts

He gave me a look of shock and delight all at once. "You're sure? I really thought this would be fun. I had no idea it was so extreme."

I stopped and brushed my thumb across his jaw. "I know, but don't worry, I'm having fun."

"I wanted to do something we always did together, but do it as your boyfriend, not just your friend. I want to make new memories with you, Jason."

"Hey, I appreciate the fact that you wanted to take me out, that you made these plans. It means a lot to me."

"I just remember how much you loved this. I thought it would be perfect."

I took a second to get my thoughts together. "I did like it, every time we've gone in the past, I've always loved it. But . . ."

Wade took my hand and waited for me to finish. The other guys seemed to realize we needed a minute, so they stood to the side and talked quietly among themselves.

"Wade, I have to make a confession. It's not an easy one for me to make, but you need to know."

He pulled me closer to him. "What is it, Jason? I thought we were good?"

"We are. We're so good. But something changed after that weekend. Not just between us. As you know, I was never afraid of anything paranormal before then. I was more interested in studying it. Finding out exactly what was causing a place to be haunted and proving it really was."

"I love that about you. I may not have loved the idea of actually seeing a ghost, but I love the time that we spend together. No matter where it is. And I love that curious nature of yours. And you know I love the gadgets." He smiled at me then, and pulled me closer, once again showing me he cared about me no matter what.

"I'm scared, Wade. I'm scared of what could happen to you if the ghosts decide that it's you they want to hurt. I'm scared of what they could do to me or what they could have done if they'd wanted to. I don't want either of us to get injured." I ran my finger along the scar on Wade's arm, remembering very clearly what had happened to him at the hands of a ghost. My throat choked with emotion, and I was having a really hard time getting out what I needed him to know. "I love you, Wade. I can't lose you over something that we don't need to do."

He leaned into me and kissed the corner of my mouth. "We do need to do it, Jason. Louise was hurting, and so was Robert. We eased their suffering by helping them cross over. They didn't mean to hurt you or me."

"I know, but he did hurt me. And he hurt you too. I wouldn't have been able to live with myself if you'd been more seriously injured while we were there. Something took over me. It was like that was all I could think of and nothing else mattered. I only cared that I helped Louise and Robert."

"Louise admitted she'd used you; she couldn't get to the basement to talk to Robert without you. But you know this."

"It was more than that. I could feel her controlling my movements, but my mind was still my own, until it wasn't. I feel like I lost that ability to block them out. When we went down into the basement in Old Town, I felt it again. They need our help, and I was powerless to stop them from taking me over. All that stopped them was that there were too many. If there had been one that was stronger, they could have taken me over and made me do whatever they wanted."

"What are you saying? Do you want to give up the ghost hunting?" Wade asked, face serious.

"I don't know. I love it, and it's amazing we can actually get paid to do it. But I won't put either of us in danger."

"What can we do for protection? There has to be something."

"There are some things; maybe we need to look into them a little deeper. So far we haven't needed them, but maybe some holy water and a box of crosses might not be such a bad idea," I joked.

Wade gave me a serious look. "If that's what it takes to keep you safe . . . to keep us all safe, then I'm for it."

"We can do some research. Maybe we can talk to a medium or a psychic, someone who might have some insight into what dangers we could really be in. Most of what I know is from a ghost hunter's perspective, not so much a spiritualist's, and that might be what we really need."

Jimbo walked over to us then, Caden and Rio right behind him. "Sorry, guys, but I heard what you were talking about. If you want to talk to someone, I can help."

"What do you mean?" I asked.

"I might know a medium," Jimbo said so quietly I had to lean in to hear him.

"What's that? You know a medium?" Wade asked.

"Yeah, she's not far from here. I can call and see if she's busy if you want to go by there tonight." He was more subdued than his regular grouchy, intense self.

"How do you know this medium?" I asked.

He looked away from us for a second before answering. "She's my sister, Janis."

"And you're just telling us this now, why?" Wade asked.

"Because it didn't matter before. Now maybe it does." He scratched his chin while he said this, seeming to be in deep thought. "Fuck it, let's go by there on the way home."

"You're not staying with us tonight; it's still our date night," Wade reminded him.

"No problem, I can hang out with your mom, Wade. She likes to cook for me when I go visit," Jimbo said with a sniff and a wave of his hand.

"Whatever. We're staying at Wade's house alone. You and his mom can have your little dinner party."

He gave me a shocked look. "Whatever, asshole." He sniffed once again. "I just happen to like hanging out with Wade's mom."

"She has a name, you know," Wade teased him mercilessly.

"I know that, but I like calling her your mom." He fought to control his smile and it came out looking more like a grimace.

I looked behind him to see Caden and Rio once again watching us with eyes full of amusement.

"Hey, don't mind us," Rio said as he pulled Caden closer into his side. "Should we move on to the next room?"

"Yes, please," Jimbo said, just a little too enthusiastically.

I put my hand on his chest to block him from leaving. "We're not done with this. You're going to take us to talk to your sister."

"I said I would, asshole. You wouldn't have even known about her if I didn't tell you."

He puffed up his chest and tried really hard to look intimidating. Which might have worked if I didn't know him. I shoved him and laughed as I walked past him.

"Come on, let's see what else this place has to offer."

Chapter Eleven

Spiders

The five of us started down the hall again, and with every step, there seemed to be more and more spider webs.

"Someone needs to call the fucking exterminator," Jimbo said under his breath.

When we finally came to the entryway for the next room, we stared. There was a cell door, metal bars that looked old but solid. It was standing ajar, and even though it should have been a clear view into the room, it was pitch black.

"Not this again. Who wants to guess what's in this one?" Wade asked.

"I hope it's not what I think it is," Caden said.

I watched Rio squeeze his hand before both of them walked closer to us.

"Just stick together. We have to be close to the end of the attraction," Wade said.

"Fuck, I hope so," Jimbo mumbled.

"Me too," Caden agreed.

I pushed open the metal door, and we moved into the room as one. It was dimly lit, but not the deep black of the earlier room. I was holding Wade's hand so tight, I had to keep reminding myself to let up and not hurt him.

Something brushed against my face, so I reached up to wipe it off, quickly realizing I'd walked right through a web.

"Watch it, guys, I just walked through a web," I warned.

"Fuck, what's that?" Caden yelled and pointed to the far corner that was so dark nothing was visible.

We froze and stared in that direction.

"I don't see anything. Are you sure you—" Wade was suddenly cut off.

A spider the size of a small car came rushing at us, its legs clattering and clicking on the floor, somehow making this whole situation even worse. It was fast too. By the time we moved to the side, it was on us. It skittered by and seemed to be in a hurry to get to something at the other end of the room.

None of us moved. Wade had his hand pressed against my stomach, holding me back against the wall, and the other three guys followed suit. We waited to see what would happen next, and we didn't have to wait long.

As my eyes adjusted to the dark, I saw every surface had webs on in. Huge webs that made it hard to know for sure what was underneath them.

We leaned away from the wall, trying to avoid touching any of the webs. I tugged Wade's hand to get him moving, and we slowly made our way in the same direction the giant spider had gone.

"Look at that." Jimbo pointed to the wall on the right.

At first, it looked like it was a wall coated with giant spider webs, but then I noticed it moving. I dropped Wade's hand as I made my way closer to it, unable to control my curiosity as to what was making it move.

I soon regretted that choice when I realized it was things caught in the webs. They squirmed and wriggled, trying to get free of their sticky prison. The masses were too big to be bugs or small animals. I walked forward and pulled some of the webbing away to see what was underneath.

Human eyes opened and a bloodcurdling scream tore from the person who was being held in a web prison by a giant spider. Logically I knew it was fake, but it didn't stop me from grabbing Wade's hand and hauling ass toward the door.

One of the guys screamed, which any other time would have been funny. But right now, all I could focus on was getting the hell out of there.

They must have felt the same because I was aware of us running as a group, full-out, to the relative safety of the door.

As soon as we were in the hall, we heard more skittering and clattering. None of us cared to look back and see where it was coming from. We were anxious to get out of here.

"Oh my god! Did you see that shit? Who thinks of these things? Fucking horrible, just horrible," Jimbo ranted, mostly to himself. But everyone agreed, no more spiders.

"We have to be close to the end. Come on, there's another door." Wade led us down the hall. I secretly hoped this room wouldn't be as bad, but I hoped that before each of them, and so far they all sucked.

I was going to be overdosing on adrenaline if there were many more surprises. Of course, much like The Vineyard House, this place just kept giving.

Chapter Twelve

Dollhouse

Now that my nerves were completely raw, it wouldn't take much to make me run out of here and never look back. Of course, I'd take Wade with me; nothing could make me leave him.

We inched our way down the hall, once again sticking close together. Somehow we ended up so close that we were shuffling our feet to avoid falling. The farther we moved from the spider room, the fewer webs were clinging to the walls and ceiling.

We stopped in front of another door, this one looked like any other door. It was wooden and had six panels. It was painted white but it was battered and the paint was peeling, either from age or use. I wasn't sure.

Wade stepped forward to turn the doorknob and I pulled him back to me.

"Nope, not this one. Let someone else do it this time."

I looked at the other three, and they looked back at me with wide eyes. Finally, Rio stepped up and turned the doorknob. We braced ourselves.

"Are you kidding me?" Jimbo asked, as he slowly stepped into what looked like a little girl's bedroom.

There were dolls everywhere. Some were torn apart and their arms and legs were dangling from the ceiling. There was a wall that was nothing but doll heads, some damaged so badly they were hard to recognize as heads. Others had creepy eyes that appeared to watch our every move. Still, others looked real.

I moved closer to get a better look, and one of them opened its eyes and looked right at me. I screamed before I even realized it and practically ran over Jimbo, trying to get away from whatever was on the wall.

"Watch it, man," Jimbo scolded.

It didn't stop me from moving away from the wall of doll heads.

"What happened?" Wade asked.

"One of them opened its eyes and looked at me."

Jimbo huffed at that and stepped closer. "Come on, man, there's no way one of these fuckers looked at you."

Just as he was about to touch one of them, a different one opened its eyes and looked at him.

"Fuck!" he yelled, as he jumped back, bumping into Caden and nearly knocking him down in his haste to get away from the doll that obviously wasn't a doll.

"I told you. Someday you'll listen to me, Jimbo," I scolded from a safe distance.

We walked around another area of the room and there was a big wardrobe that looked like a person or two could fit in it. None of us took the time to look into it; none of us were too interested in knowing what was inside.

The other side of the room was a big pile of doll parts. All of them broken and torn apart. There was every type of doll in that pile. From baby dolls to the large dolls a little girl could have as a pretend friend.

"You guys ready to get out of here?" Caden asked, sounding nervous.

"Yeah, I'm ready to go," Rio answered with a soft smile and a tug on his hand.

We turned around to go back toward the door, when suddenly the pile of doll parts started moving. A person, made up to look like a mannequin, climbed out from under the legs, arms, and other doll pieces. We froze as another mannequin sat up and teetered its way toward us.

"What the fuck?" Jimbo, always so eloquent.

"What he said," Rio agreed. "Let's get out of here."

He started walking toward the door, tugging Caden along behind him. As he passed the cabinet, the door swung open and a group of mannequins started piling out of it.

"Time to go," Wade said, his voice panicked.

We backed out of the room now, none of us willing to turn our back on the creepy spectacle of living dolls.

There were around ten of them, all looking like they'd been through hell and back. Some were even partially burned, and all of them had the same blank expression as they slowly made their way to us.

"Open the door, Rio," Jimbo yelled. "I'm out of here."

If it had been any other situation, I probably would've laughed at his reaction. But this was weird as hell, and I had no more patience for being scared to death. We broke into a run as soon as the door swung open, nearly bowling over Rio and Caden in our rush to get out of there.

Rio slammed the door shut as soon as Wade was clear and slumped down to the floor.

"Are you okay?" Caden asked, voice full of concern.

"Yeah, baby. That just scared the shit out of me. Promise me, no more dolls—ever."

Caden held his hand out to help him up.

"Sounds good to me," he said with a visible shiver.

Wade slipped his arm around my waist and held me close as we walked down the hall. Suddenly the door opened and one of the mannequins peeked their head out, slowly turning until it could see us. With an evil grin, it waved at us.

That got us moving.

Chapter Thirteen

Exit

A little further down the hall, there was a big exit sign, right next to a double door. I breathed a sigh of relief as we moved toward it.

There was a flashing to the right of the exit, like a television screen that was reflecting on the surrounding walls. I didn't immediately look that way, too intent on going through that door and getting out of here.

Jimbo suddenly stopped right in front of me, and I bounced off his back.

"What are you doing? Let's go."

He didn't say anything, only pointed away from the door.

There was a giant flat screen television mounted in the center of the wall. It took up most of the area and illuminated the room. The television didn't seem to be playing anything; it was just snow.

Then I noticed something coming into focus on the screen. I looked over at Wade and he must've seen it too because he leaned forward like he was trying to get a closer look.

Jimbo had his arms crossed over his body and looked even more nervous than he had a few minutes ago. Caden and Rio were staring at the screen too.

Somehow this was familiar to me. I'd seen this play out in some way before. In a blink, there was a girl with long hair covering her face standing in the middle of the screen.

"Oh fuck, not that," Rio said, fearful. "Come on, Caden, let's go. I'm done."

I looked over and saw him tugging on Caden's hand. But Caden was still watching the screen. I turned to look at it and saw the girl was now much closer to the edge. The image flashed a few times, and suddenly she was at the very front.

I glanced back at Wade and he looked at me before we both looked back at the screen. Just like in the movie, the girl started climbing out of the television screen. In her full creepy likeness, her hair long and stringy, hiding her face.

She contorted herself and pulled her leg up to an impossible angle and proceeded to slink right out of the television screen. That was all it took to get me in motion. I turned to the exit and tugged on Wade's hand to get him to follow.

Caden and Rio were already gone. Jimbo stood close to the exit with his arms crossed, impatient as ever. I tugged again, but Wade didn't move.

"Come on, Wade, let's get out of here." I turned to see why he wasn't moving. Only it wasn't Wade, it was the fucking girl from the screen.

"Holy shit!" I shouted and dropped her hand like I was burned.

I looked over to see Jimbo bent over laughing at me, and when I turned back to the girl, her hair was now parted around her face, and she was laughing too. Standing right next to her was Wade.

I walked up to him and punched him in the shoulder. "What the hell, Wade?"

"Oh my god, Jason. This is Maya from my work. She told me she was playing the girl from The Ring at the end of the attraction, and I couldn't resist setting this up. Sorry, I know it was totally cruel, but I couldn't resist."

My mouth hung open, hearing him explain he'd planned this. I had to admit, it was genius.

"You know you're going to pay for this, right?"

He laughed out loud at that. "I knew it. But it was so worth it. I never get the chance to put one over on you."

I gave him a playful shove. "Just remember that the next time I pull one over on you. Payback's a bitch."

"Sorry, I'm Maya. Like Wade said, we work together. I usually work at one of the haunted house attractions every year." She held her hand out for me to shake.

"Jason. Nice to meet you, Maya. Not gonna lie, I wish it would have been under other circumstances. Wade knows that movie really creeped me out."

She laughed at that. "I'm really sorry, I just went along thinking he knew what he was doing."

"Oh, he knew exactly what he was doing."

I swung my arm around his shoulders and pulled him to me, kissing the side of his head.

"You are so going to pay, just so you know," I reminded him.

"I know, but yeah, totally worth it. Let's go. I think Caden and Rio must be halfway to Reno by now."

I laughed at that, and after saying goodnight to Maya, we walked toward the exit.

"So, what did you think of that, Jason?" Jimbo asked, wearing the smirk of someone who was also in on the joke.

I punched him in the arm as I walked by. "Oh, it was great. But like I told Wade, payback's a bitch."

He laughed while rubbing his arm. "Totally worth it."

"You two really are assholes," I grumbled as we finally exited the building.

Rio and Caden were standing off to the side and walked up to us. "What happened? I thought you guys were right behind us," Caden said.

"We were, but then Wade thought it would be funny to play a joke on me."

Rio looked between the two of us, shocked. "You did not play a joke on him that involved the creepy chick from The Ring."

"Yep, I totally did." And he proceeded to tell them about how he'd planned it out and how it had scared me to death.

"Man, that's not right." Rio gave Wade a look that would have been threatening if he hadn't immediately started laughing.

"Thanks for the support, Rio." I patted him on the back while he fought for control.

He wiped the tears from his eyes from laughing so hard. "Dude, I would have screamed and ran. I probably would have left Caden to fend for himself." He looked over at his boyfriend and gave him a warm look before leaning in to kiss him softly. "Probably not."

Caden smiled back at him and pulled him in for a hug. "You won't get rid of me that easy," he joked.

"You guys are too easy. I wouldn't have stuck around long enough for her to grab me," Jimbo bragged while puffing out his chest.

Wade and I dissolved into laughter.

"Let's get going. Did you want go to your sister's?" I asked Jimbo.

He thought about it for a second before he answered. "Yes, but just consider yourself warned, she's a little different."

"Okay, whatever that means. Like more different than you are?" I smiled at him.

"Fucker, let's get going." He marched off in the direction of the carpark.

"Nice meeting you guys, we should meet up again sometime." Wade shook hands with Rio and Caden and they exchanged phone numbers. I waved to them as we followed Jimbo out.

Chapter Fourteen

Beacon

Jimbo was standing there waiting impatiently.

"Where's your car?"

"I left it at Wade's house; I told you this earlier."

I shook my finger in his face. "You're not staying at Wade's house. We told you this is our date night."

He pushed my finger away. "I know, fucker. Let's get this over with."

When we got to the car, we piled in and drove to the nearest onramp for I-80. Jimbo gave directions to Wade from the back.

"It's not far. She lives in the downtown area in one of the older houses."

He directed us to take the exit that was closest to the hospital, and then we ended up in a residential area.

"So, what's this about, Jimbo? Why didn't you tell us about your sister before?"

"There wasn't a reason to. She's a little intense, so I try not to get into ghost shit with her. To be honest, she kinda freaks me out. When we were kids, she'd get this blank look on her face and start talking about other people being in the room that I couldn't see."

"Whoa, we could have used her at The Vineyard House," Wade said.

"She can't control it. Not all of them reveal themselves to her. And some of them have attacked her in the past. She says it's what she's meant to do. To be a conduit between our world and theirs. But she has no control over them."

"How can she help then?"

"She can block them. She's gone for years with not contacting them and not letting them use her. She's different than you, Jason. She can see them and hear them. To her they appear as human as you and me. When she was young, she didn't realize they weren't alive and only she could see them."

We continued to drive, following his directions, until we saw a huge illuminated hand in front of one of the houses on a small street.

"That's her on the left." He pointed at the big hand.

Wade parked right in front and waited for Jimbo to tell us what to do next. He looked really unsure about going in.

"You sure this is a good idea?" I asked again.

"Yeah, you need to have someone teach you some ways to protect yourself, and she can do that."

We walked up to the door and Jimbo knocked.

"Come in, James," a woman called from inside.

Wade and I both looked at Jimbo and smirked.

"James?" I whispered. Wade snickered, only partially containing his laughter.

"Shut it, asshole," Jimbo snipped, while turning the doorknob.

We followed him into the entry and waited for him to introduce us to his sister.

"Hello, everyone, I'm Janis." She walked over to us from the small kitchen. She looked exactly like Jimbo but with hair long enough to tell it was a light blonde. She had the same light blue eyes and warm smile. It was eerie how much they resembled each other.

"You're Wade, the empath." She shook Wade's hand while she said this and then turned to me.

"You're Jason. You've always been aware of spirits. You recently found out that they can communicate with you and take you over. You want to know how you can protect yourself and your boyfriend from harm."

"Ye—Ahem, yeah. How did you know?" I stammered before finally spitting out the words.

She gave me a serene, all-knowing smile. "I know a lot of things. Don't I, James?"

He glanced away from her before giving her an intense look I didn't understand.

"Yes, Janis. You've always known too much," he said.

"That's true, but that brings us to why you're here to begin with. Jason, I can show you how to put up a psychic wall around yourself and others to protect you from the influence of the spirits."

"How will I do that though? I have no clue if I even can."

"You can. The ability you have to contact them and interact with them is not a one-way door. You can also close that door and lock it whenever you need to. You just need to know how."

"Really, you'd show me? Th—thank you, I don't want to put any of us in danger."

She smiled at me again with that overly calm expression.

"I can show you, but you'll need to put a protective wall around James too. As long as he's with you, the spirits will seek you all out."

I whipped my head around to look at Jimbo, who was pale and had a guilty look on his face.

"What's she talking about, Jimbo?"

Janis didn't offer any more information. She just looked calmly at each of us in turn.

"Jimbo?" Wade tried.

He shuffled from foot to foot before shooting a glare at his sister. She smiled in return.

"James, they need to know." She pushed a little more.

His eyes bore into hers, and finally he looked away.

"What's she talking about, Jimbo?" I whispered.

"I'm a beacon," Jimbo said, barely loud enough for us to hear.

"A what? I don't understand." I looked between Jimbo and Janis, hoping someone would explain exactly what was going on.

Wade stepped closer to me and slipped his arm around my back. I glanced quickly at him, and then my focus was back on Jimbo.

"My brother has the ability to attract spirits. They see him as a beacon in the night. If he's near them, they'll seek him out. He doesn't have the ability to interact with them, so this angers them. But he can't help it and he can't change it. All he can do is try to dim his light."

I stared at Jimbo in shock. "Why didn't you tell us this?"

"It makes no difference. I can't communicate with them."

"It makes a hell of a lot of difference. What if you're the reason Louise decided to make her presence known?" I said.

"He didn't make her interact with you. The spirits at The Vineyard House had been there for many years before any of you were even born. She was drawn to James, as were other spirits in the house. But they couldn't communicate with him the way they can with you.

Louise came to him in dreams, but he couldn't help her. Not like you and Wade did. The three of you together can do more than any of you can alone."

Wade and I shared a look; we were both on the same page. Like we always had been. He gave me a slight nod and we both looked at Jimbo to find him giving us an uncertain gaze.

"You can help? Show us how to block them from attacking? And how to control their interactions with us?"

She once again gave each of us that warm smile.

"I can, and I will. You're all meant to help them. But you need to learn how to protect yourselves."

Wade squeezed me closer to his side, and I knew this was something we had to do if we were going to continue to help any spirits that were trapped here.

"When can we begin?" I asked. Jimbo's head snapped up, and he looked at us.

"We?" he asked.

"Jimbo, you're one of us. We'll figure it out together. Then we'll help whatever spirits we can."

Janis smiled, and with her hands held in front of her, she asked, "Are you ready to begin now?"

"Yeah, we are," I answered, more sure now than I had been before. Like Louise Chalmers said, we were stronger together.

The End

About the Author

BL Maxwell grew up in a small town listening to her grandfather spin tales about his childhood. Later she became an avid reader and after a certain vampire series she became obsessed with fanfiction. She soon discovered Slash fanfiction and later discovered the MM genre and was hooked. Many years later, she decided to take the plunge and write down some of the stories that seem to run through her head late at night when she's trying to sleep.

Contact:

Email: blmaxwell.writer@gmail.com
https://smart.bio/blmaxwellwriter/

Also By L Maxwell

Thank you for reading Ghost Haunted. All books in this series are based on real hauntings in or around Sacramento California.

VALLEY GHOSTS series

Series Link: mybook.to/ValleyGhostsSeries

Ghost Hunted

Ghost Haunted

Ghost Trapped

Ghost Hexed

Ghost Handled

Ghost Shadow

Haunting Destiny

Green Eyed Boy, Lobster Tales Book One, is available Here:

https://mybook.to/GreenEyedBoy

Two strangers, drawn together over their work ethic, and sealing the deal over delicious lobster rolls. They could just be the perfect match.

After quitting his job, Billie Watts hits all the food festivals he can as he drives across the country. When he finally reaches Stoney Brook, Maine, he's excited to find he's there just in time to try one of the lobster rolls he's heard so much about. The bright neon yellow food truck with a giant red lobster on top looks like the perfect place to try it.

Lance Karl is as ready as he can be for the start of the three-day Tall Ships Festival and hopes to sell enough lobster rolls out of his food truck to make a good start towards owning a restaurant. The day begins cold and misty, and a text from his nephew saying he can't help him is not the perfect start he'd hoped for.

When a green-eyed stranger interrupts his frantic morning, Lance doesn't realize meeting Billie will not only change his day, but maybe even the rest of his life. Two strangers, drawn together over their work ethic, and sealing the deal over delicious lobster rolls. They could just be the perfect match. A small-town MM Vacation romance.#friends to lovers #meetcute #workplace romance #mm romance

Enjoy a Free copy of Try To Remember. A short story with Andy and Link.

https://blmaxwellwriter.com/free-reads/

And a Free copy of A Night To Remember. A short story with Sam and Erik.

https://books2read.com/u/baDrw8

Preorder The Things We Lose: https://mybook.to/TTWLose

BETTER TOGETHER series

Better Together

Chains Required

The First Twelve

The Better Together Boxset

THE STONE series

Stone Under Skin

Blood Beneath Stone

Stone Hearts

The Stone Series Box Set

SMALL TOWN CITY series

Remember When

A Night to Remember (Short Story)

Try To Forget

Try To Remember (Short Story)

One Last Chance

CONSORTIUM TRILOGY

Burning Addiction

Freezing Aversion

FOUR PACKS Trilogy

The Slow Death

The Ultimate Sacrifice

The Final Salvation

STANDALONE

The List

Double Black Diamonds

Ride: The Chance of a Lifetime

Check Yes or No

A Ghost of a Chance

Tutu

Salt & Lime

Amos Ridge

Six Months

Ten or Fifteen Miles

The Snake in the Castle

Green Eyed Boy

A Beach Far Away

The Things We Find

Blinding Light

Peppermint Mocha Kisses

Small Town City Series

Remember When

BL Maxwell
https://mybook.to/RememberWhenA
A night to remember, a confession, and a lifetime of love in this small town, friends to lovers Christmas romance.
Andrew Lawson's life in Sacramento has turned from being everything he dreamed of growing up, to a lonely place where finding someone special to share his life with is impossible. When the first person he meets on returning home for Thanksgiving is his childhood friend Link, it's a reminder of happier times when his whole future lay in front of him. Agreeing to a drink before heading to his parent's place is a way to reconnect, and a great way to start the holiday.
Link Stanton never considered leaving the small farming town he grew up in, but he misses Andy more than he'll ever admit. Secretly lusting after a friend is bad enough but being in love with him is so much worse. One drink with friends seems harmless enough, after all, catching up on old times can't be a bad thing, until beers turn to shots, and Link reveals how he really feels.
Everything could change, and if Andrew doesn't remember Link's heartfelt confession, they could carry on as friends. But, if he does remember, this could be either the worst, or the best, Christmas of all. #smalltownromance #Holidayromance #mmromance #Christmas #friendstolovers

Try To Forget

BL Maxwell

https://mybook.to/TryToForget
After being dumped by his boyfriend, spending the weekend alone wasn't something Sam Braun was looking forward to. So, when the hairstylist that works next to his bookstore invites him to his hometown for the weekend, Sam jumps at the chance. Visiting the small town of Occident could be just what he needs to forget, at least for a few days.
Erik Thorne has lived his whole life in the same town where nothing new ever happens, and any stranger who comes to town is always a big deal. When his old friend Andy brings a friend home for the weekend, Erik is drawn to the man in a way that confuses him at first. But his curiosity about the gorgeous blond from the city gets the better of him, and he can't resist spending more time with him.
Sam was hoping to forget his troubles when he meets Erik. While Erik can't seem to think of anything besides the city boy with the bookstore he can't wait to visit. Distance might not be the only thing that stands between them, as they find out admitting what you want isn't always easy. Each book can be read as a standalone. #AgeGap, #MMRomance, #FriendsToLovers #OppositesAttract #SmallTownRomance #City/Country

One Last Chance (New Release)

https://mybook.to/OLCSmalltown
Stu Lawson had always lived in the small town of Occident. He'd been born a farmer, and he was more than happy to stay a farmer even when his dad decided it wasn't the life for him. He's been raising his daughter since the day she was born, and he's never regretted being a single dad, but Stu has a few secrets.

Morgan Grant was born into a life he never wanted and had done everything he could to avoid. Staying drunk helps him forget and numbs the pain he can't bring himself to face. After a long night of drinking, he ends up dumped in a small town north of Sacramento without money, his phone, or a way to get back to the city he calls home.

Stu's focus has always been his daughter, but he can't control his curiosity about the stranger who shows up in Occident alone in the middle of the night. He offers to help, even when he knows he shouldn't. Old feelings rise to the surface and he's helpless to ignore them, or Morgan. This stranger could be his chance at happiness, or his downfall. #singledad #gayromance #stranded #smalltownromance #secrets

Peppermint Mocha Kisses

https://mybook.to/PeppermintMK

Randy Miller wants nothing more than to make a living selling the fantastic cookies he dreams up when he's not working as a web designer. He's always loved baking, but he's afraid of taking the leap from hobby to business. Mostly he's afraid of failing, and of Eli coming up with a better recipe.

Eli Canton has a crush. A big crush on someone who avoids him whenever he can. Eli loves everything about Randy, even if he's grouchy and seems to work way too much. Eli knows he's not all bad and hopes to have a chance with him someday.

A broken oven throws the two of them together, and even though Randy doesn't want to admit it, he likes the time he spends with Eli. And Eli definitely can't wait to spend more time with Randy. Now if only they can make it past the annual cookie exchange and possibly Valentine's Day to their own sweet happy ending. #smalltown Romance, #opposites attract, #MM Romance

The Ultimate Sacrifice (Four Packs Trilogy Book 2)

https://mybook.to/FourPacksTrilogy

Grady Summerville is facing a slow and agonizing death, but has come to terms with his disease and doesn't fear dying. However, fate has other ideas, presenting him with a future thanks to Max Steele. Grady owes his very life to Max, and as his health improves, finds himself falling head over heels with his savior.

Max Steele has been forced to leave his pack and everyone he knows to move to the West Territory to be a blood donor for Grady. He knows it's the right thing to do, but it doesn't mean he has to like it.

As tensions escalate between the two packs, Max finds his loyalty tested and is torn between following his alpha, or following his heart.

If Max doesn't make the sacrifice then it will be Grady making the ultimate sacrifice and paying with his life. #MMParanormal #Shifters

Freezing Aversion (Consortium Trilogy Book Two)

The cold isn't the only killer in the wilderness.

https://mybook.to/FreezingAversion

Benjamin Coulton is a tracker employed by the Consortium, the ruling counsel of vampires. When he's sent to investigate a rogue vampire killing indiscriminately in a remote region of Alaska. Bad weather hampers his effort and he loses the vampire he's been tasked to find.

Leon Davis and his friend Trevor agreed to be winter caretakers for several cabins and a fishing lodge, thinking it would be easy money. They settle into their daily routine of checking the cabins for animal break-ins, or broken water pipes, and prepare for a long winter.

Until a run in with a vampire changes everything.

Ben finds a newly turned vampire left for dead by the rogue vampire, and suddenly Ben's mission changes course. In the freezing wilderness of Alaska, he uncovers more truths and the mate he'd always longed for... and now the vampire he was tasked to find is hunting them. #MMParanormalRomance #vampire #fatedmate #thriller

A Ghost of a Chance

https://mybook.to/AGhostOfAChance

James McKinney has always lived life alone. He doesn't have a family, at least none that he remembers. He's always dreamed of having a house of his own, a place he can call home. Finding the right house, ready to work to make it his home, nothing can put a damper on his happiness, or can it?Trey Andral, returning home from college, notices someone moving into his old friend's house next door. Miss Hattie is still waving to him from the bedroom window, even though he knows she's gone. He also knows he can't not help the new guy make the house his own.Trey has always been able to see and hear sprits, but what's normal to him is terrifying to most others. When the spirits seem intent on contacting James, Trey has no choice but to share his secret, risking their friendship. If they work together, maybe they can figure out what the clues the spirits are giving them mean. And maybe they can find family in each other.

Tutu (Malicious Gods: Egypt)

https://mybook.to/Tutu

Kit Nelson was thrown into the world of demons and cults as a child. He's learned to depend on no one, and to do all he can to keep himself safe from dark forces. He also knows he can't trust anyone else with his life. He knows what the demons who hunt him have in mind for him, and he'll fight it every step of the way.

Tommy Smythe and his sister Lola have been fighting what they know is a rising tide of evil for years. They're prepared with all their paranormal weaponry, including the assistance of an ancient god who has fought demons his whole existence. Tutu, the Egyptian god and Master of Demons has chosen Tommy to be his vessel and his sword when needed to destroy any and all demons.

A new threat ripples through the dark underworld, one that will be felt across all mankind. A demon has chosen one whose body he will use to return to the land of the living. But only if Kit, Tommy, and Lola can't stop him. Only Tutu has the power and knowledge to protect them from the demon Rerek, and he also knows even with his help, this is not going to be an easy battle.

Amos Ridge

https://mybook.to/AmosRidge

"There's no time. Remember, I love you."It all started with a discovery. A cave beneath a waterfall that held a crystal. Two boys—best friends—embark on a journey they're told will help all mankind. As the years go by, their friendship turns to love, and their adventure turns into a battle.Drew Langly is the keeper of the crystal. With his contact, the crystal allows them to jump to different timestreams and help, if they can, to further that society or fix anything that improves their lives. When he's ripped from the timestream, it's the beginning of what will change everything they've come to know about how the different timestreams function.Colby Adams is Drew's boyfriend, fellow traveler, and jump partner. When Drew is left vulnerable after a failed jump, he's there to help and try to figure out what went wrong. They soon discover another team of travelers is in trouble, but they've been warned against trusting them. The more they learn, the more they realize everything has been a lie. To rewrite a history that's been full of deceit, they'll need to put their trust, once again, in strangers. Can they rewind it all and begin again? Experience the history they were always meant to? With some unconventional help, maybe...Amos Ridge is the fifth book in the multi-author series, Beyond the Realm: Remember. Each book is set in its own world and can be read as a standalone novel. Join eight authors on eight very different, romantic, and magical stories as each one writes their own take on the same concept.

www.ingramcontent.com/pod-product-compliance
Ingram Content Group UK Ltd.
Pitfield, Milton Keynes, MK11 3LW, UK
UKHW041844200726
13854UKWH00005BA/2066